W9-DDJ-415

CELEBRATING U.S. HOLIDAYS

Why Do We Celebrate VETERANS DAY?

Grace Houser

PowerKiDS press.

New York

Published in 2019 by The Rosen Publishing Group, Inc.
29 East 21st Street, New York, NY 10010

First Edition

Editor: Brianna Battista
Book Design: Reann Nye

Photo Credits: Cover ESB Professional/Shutterstock.com; p. 5 Anthony Correia/Shutterstock.com; p. 6 Sean Pavone/Shutterstock.com; p. 9 Andrew Burton/Getty Images News/Getty Images; p. 10 michaeljung/Shutterstock.com; p. 13 Paula Bronstein/Getty Images News/Getty Images; p. 14 Terry Vine/J Patrick Lane/Blend Images/Getty Images; p. 17 a katz/Shutterstock.com; p. 18 Archistoric/Alamy Stock Photo; p. 21 MANDEL NGAN/AFP/Getty Images; p. 23 Evgeniy Kalinovskiy/Shutterstock.com.

Cataloging-in-Publication Data

Names: Houser, Grace.
Title: Why do we celebrate Veterans Day? / Grace Houser.
Description: New York : PowerKids Press, 2019. | Series: Celebrating U.S. holidays | Includes index.
Identifiers: LCCN ISBN 9781508166733 (pbk.) | ISBN 9781508166719 (library bound) | ISBN 9781508166740 (6 pack)
Subjects: LCSH: Veterans Day-Juvenile literature.
Classification: LCC D671.H68 2019 | DDC 394.264-dc23

Manufactured in the United States of America

CPSIA Compliance Information: Batch #CS18PK: For Further Information contact Rosen Publishing, New York, New York at 1-800-237-9932

CONTENTS

Veterans Day is on November 11 each year.

5

6

Fighting in World War I ended on this day in 1918.

7

Veterans Day honors American soldiers of the past and present.

9

Soldiers serve in the armed forces.

11

The armed forces are the Air Force, Army, Coast Guard, Marine Corps, and Navy.

13

Soldiers serve during times of war. They also serve during times of peace.

People fly **flags** on Veterans Day. Many cities have **parades**.

17

Birmingham, Alabama, holds the oldest Veterans Day parade each year.

People thank soldiers on Veterans Day. They may also visit **memorials**.

20

21

22

Do you know any veterans?
Remember to thank them for
their service!

23

Words to Know

flags

memorial

parade

Index

Websites

Due to the changing nature of Internet links, PowerKids Press has developed an online list of websites related to the subject of this book. This site is updated regularly. Please use this link to access the list: www.powerkidslinks.com/ushol/vets